If Only I Had Listened To My Mom

Written by: Tanice Amira Simmons

Written by: Tanice Amira Simmons
Illustrated by: Shanzay Noor

This book belongs to:

____

Beep beep beep! That's the sound of my alarm clock. It wakes me up each morning to start the day.

Pretty cool right?

My mom gives me a set of rules to follow each day. Today she told me to clean up my mess after breakfast; but I forgot and began playing with my bouncy ball, when suddenly...

I accidentally bounced the ball so hard, it landed on the breakfast table and spilled my leftover milk mom had asked me to clean up.

If only I had listened to my mom...

After I cleaned up the spill, mom helped me put on my shoes to go outside for a walk. She told me to stay close, so she could keep an eye on me.

As we were walking, I noticed a group of birds and started to chase them away! I can hear my mom yell "slow down!"

When suddenly...

I fell down and scraped my leg on the ground! "Ouch that really hurts".

If only I had listened to my mom.

It was time to go inside for a snack. Mom always says to wash your hands before eating.

I was so excited to eat the yummy cookies mom put out, I forgot to wash the germs away.

Hand
Soap

Later that day I started to feel really sick! Could it be because I didn't wash my hands?

If only I had listened to my mom.

About the Author

Hi Tanice here!

Thank you for taking the time to read my very first children's book. Being a full time mom and running my own business can be a handful. There's nothing I enjoy more than watching my daughter grow up to becoming the best version of herself, through all the lessons life brings and of course anything I am able to teach. I wrote this book to make story time enjoyable, relatable and a great learning tool for our little ones.

I hope you and your family enjoyed reading as much as I enjoyed writing. Until next time.